For my parents and my sister, Valerie, who continue to be there to cheer me on. Much love to Laura Numeroff for guiding me along the way and Brian Martin for bringing my book to life.

Every morning, Ruby wakes up excited and looks forward to jumping and skipping on her way to school.

SCHOOL ZONE

Every afternoon, she looks forward to spreading her arms and embracing the rays of the golden sun.

Every night, Ruby peers out her window and feels the glow of the moon upon her sleepy face and frazzled hair.

Every day, Ruby is absolutely certain that her days will fill her with new friends and unforgettable memories.

Ruby is unique, and she loves it!

While everyone at school wants to be engineers, nurses, lawyers, teachers, police officers or firefighters, Ruby hopes to be a singer, dancer, writer and actor!

Ruby loves being unique. At lunch, Ruby asks her friends, "What's your favorite thing in the whole wide world?"

"Ice cream!" says Valerie.

"Coloring!" says Jeremy.

"Chicken nuggets!" says Melonie.

"My puppy!" says Emily.

Ruby knows she enjoys these things, but even more she knows she cannot live without the music she sings and dances along to and her imagination, which inspires her to be anything and anyone she wants.

Ruby's favorite thing in the whole wide world is being a performer on stage for all eyes to see.

Ruby knows her talent, dedication, and vibrant personality make her stand out.

Ruby absolutely adores mixing and matching her wardrobe, playing with hairstyles, and strutting with shoes that compliment her personality.

Today is a special day for Ruby because she is finally going to learn how to swim.

"I will be able to glide beautifully on stage if I know how to swim. Let's go get a bathing suit!" she says to her mother.

As soon as Ruby steps into the store, she is welcomed by a parade of colors. Coral pinks, deep greens, vibrant purples, brilliant yellows, radiant oranges, and royal blues, too! Ruby has so many choices! There are floral, stripes, polka dots, stars, and zigzags.

"Hmm, what will make me stand out? What will make me shine when I am out and about? What shows I'm unique?"

Ruby grabs a yellow bikini with sparkly red ladybugs.

As Ruby stands on her tippy toes, she holds the bathing suit. With a smile that glows, she says, "This one is unique just like me."

Ruby is so excited to show off her new bathing suit that when she arrives at the pool, she is the first one out and ready on the pool deck.

"Ruby!" says Valerie.

Ruby hugs her best friend who is also
taking swimming lessons.

Ruby and Valerie are filled with so much
excitement that they both start jumping,
dancing, singing and prancing.

"Where's your button?"
Valerie asked curiously.

Ruby knows that her button is missing, but she really hopes it will grow one day.

Will it grow into a dot like the one on her mom's belly, or will it grow into something easier to spot? Will it grow with polka dots? Ruby wonders. Will it grow into a bright yellow button? Will it grow into a button with stripes or zigzags?

Ruby knows that her button is missing, but really hopes it will grow one day, and so she says, "It's still growing."

Standing amid sandals, lifeguards, and wet footprints on the concrete, she notices that every boy and girl has a button. Everyone, but Ruby, has a button on their belly.

Maybe Ruby already had
a button but lost it.

So, Ruby and Valerie begin to look
everywhere for her missing little button.

For the first time, Ruby wants to hide. For the first time, she feels that all eyes are staring, not admiring her. For the first time, she does not want to stand out. For the first time, she does not want to be unique.

Shoulders slouched, head hanging down, Ruby feels the heat of embarrassment rushing to her face as she says to herself, "I'll always be missing my button."

As Ruby sits at the edge of the pool,
Valerie sits right next to her and says...
"What about your singing?"
"What about your acting?"
"What about your dancing?"

"What about your stories and writing? They never left your side.
You never needed your button before."

Ruby's face begins to lighten! The more she appreciates herself, the more she loves herself. The more she loves herself, the more she embraces her passion, which will always be there to make her happy.

"Ruby, even without your button you will never be forgotten. You will always be unique."

A young girl named Ruby was born without her little belly button. She was born with a voice that will never be forgotten, toes that help her prance here and there, and a heart that chases every deepest desire. Ruby is unique and she loves it.

Made in the USA
Coppell, TX
08 December 2023

25659754R00017